# MAFIA DADDY

## A BAD BOY ROMANCE

RENEE ROSE

This book was originally published in the USA Today Bestselling anthology *Daddy's Demands*.

Published in the United States of America

Renee Rose Romance

Editor: Jamie with Stormy Night Publications

This e-book is a work of fiction. While reference might be made to actual historical events or existing locations, the names, characters, places and incidents are either the product of the author's imaginations or are used fictitiously, and any resemblance to actual persons, living or dead, business establishments, events, or locales is entirely coincidental.

This book contains descriptions of many BDSM and sexual practices, but this is a work of fiction and, as such, should not be used in any way as a guide. The author and publisher will not be responsible for any loss, harm, injury, or death resulting from use of the information contained within. In other words, don't try this at home, folks!

# WANT FREE RENEE ROSE BOOKS?

# CHAPTER 1

 enna

THE POUNDING MUSIC might be the only thing keeping me on my feet at the moment. I bounce and spin on the dance floor to the beats of DJ Sunshine, the coolest female DJ on Ibiza. I may or may not have one too many cosmos in me. The room tilts and spins alarmingly every time I slow down.

I guess I ought to thank mobster Nico Tacone for footing the bill on this party lifestyle, but I spent my entire life hating him, so gratitude would be an adjustment. Still, he released me from our marriage contract and gave me the money to run away until he worked things out with our families, so I have nothing to complain about.

I turn and run into a wall of fine Italian suit. Pleasure overtakes me at a familiar masculine scent, and I throw my arms around the man's neck before my brain registers what this means.

I've been found. Caught.

"Alex!" I breathe.

My father's right-hand man. His soldier, bodyguard, protégé—whatever you want to call him.

I don't mean to fling myself at him, but my body control isn't the best. Oh, who am I kidding? I totally want to plaster myself all over this man.

He's been the subject of my schoolgirl crushes since I was fifteen.

Strong, handsome, powerful, sexy. Italian. He's everything I love in a man. And he's off limits. Or rather, as a mafia princess with a marriage contract to another family, *I've* been off limits to him.

Which meant no matter how much I flirted or attempted to provoke him, he never showed any interest beyond the smolder of desire I swore burned in his gaze. But then, he might give every girl those sizzling looks, because I'm pretty sure he's a huge player.

His iron arm bands around my waist, presumably to hold me up, since I'm not doing a great job of it myself, but I take it as an invitation and lift my legs to wrap around his waist.

"That's it, *bambina.*" He's never called me *baby* before and the pleasure of it ripples through me as he shifts his forearm under my ass, turns and walks swiftly toward the door.

By the time my brain catches on to what's happening,

we're off the dance floor and almost out of the nightclub. "Wait!" I try to get down. I guess when I attached myself to him in greeting, I was angling for some sexy dancing out on the floor. But Alex is all business, and if he thinks he's dragging me back to Chicago to face my father, he's going to have a fight on his hands.

I kick and thrash and suddenly Yuri, the huge, tattooed Russian who sits and watches the DJ, Lucy, every night with a moon face, steps in front of us, blocking Alex.

"Put girl down." His accent is as thick as his meaty arms.

You gotta love Yuri. I'm ninety-nine point nine percent sure he's ex-mafia, too. Or *bratva*—whatever they call Russian *mafiya*. His tattoos read like a rap sheet and when he's not looking moony at Lucy, his expression promises death to anyone who gets in his way or looks too long at his girl.

Alex's body, already rigid, goes even tighter. He lowers me slowly to my feet, I suppose so he has his hands free to fight.

I thrust my body between them, but Alex effortlessly pushes me behind him.

"It's okay, Yuri." Damn, I'm slurring a bit. I pat Alex's well-dressed arm. "He's mine. I mean—he's with me. I'm with him. He can take me now."

Yuri cracks his knuckles. "You know this guy? He's not safe."

I actually hear Alex growl beside me.

"He's safe for me," I say quickly. "Not for other people." *Definitely not for you.* I take Alex's arm, anxious to get out of there without any bloodshed. "Let us pass, Yuri."

Yuri's eyes narrow, but after two beats, he steps aside.

Alex doesn't take his menacing glare off the guy until we're long past, then he swoops me back up, carrying me toddler style on his hip.

"This is fun." I sit even taller and kick my feet like a happy tot. It's a ridiculous position, but I love it.

"I would throw you over my fucking shoulder, but I'm afraid you'd puke on my heels," Alex grumbles.

I giggle and tangle my fingers in his thick, dark hair. Somewhere in the back of my mind, I already know I'm going to be embarrassed about my behavior tomorrow, but in this moment, it's too pleasurable to be this close to Alex with my inhibitions down.

Apparently he's cased me out, because he walks the block back to my hotel and goes straight to my suite, where he waits for me to fumble in the tiny cross-shoulder purse for the key. I accidentally drop it and only then does he put me down.

I'm drunk, so I'm probably making stuff up, but I like to think he enjoyed carrying me as much as I loved straddling his waist. Of course, I'd like to straddle his waist in a whole different configuration, but that probably won't happen.

"Please tell me my dad isn't here," I slur as he unlocks the door to the luxury suite I've been staying in and pushes it open.

"Nope, just me." His voice is tight. He takes off his suit jacket with an impatient jerk.

"Why are you pissed?"

He cocks a brow, which is an extremely sexy look on him. I definitely have a thing for pissed-off Italian hot

4

shots. Casualty of living in *La Cosa Nostra*, I guess. His eyes rake over me, taking in my short mini-skirt and cropped spaghetti top.

Okay, I'm showing way more skin than I would back home, but I'm on a Spanish island.

"You were dancing at a nightclub, dressed like that —*drunk*. Anything could've happened to you, *piccolina*!"

I shake my head, which has the effect of making the room spin. "I was safe," I slur. "You saw how Yuri act—"

I'm cut off when Alex grabs my forearm, spins me around, and pushes my torso down over the bed. I giggle when his hand smacks down on my ass, even though it smarts like hell.

"Don't say that fucking name again."

"What? Yuri—*ow*! Okay! Ouch." I dance right and left as he smacks my ass five more times. "Jesus, Alex. What— are you jealous?" Again, it's something I wouldn't have said sober. But I've also never been bent over and spanked by my father's soldier either.

And I have to say, it's thrilling, albeit a bit stingy.

I'm not afraid of Alex. I meant what I said to Yuri— he's safe for me. His loyalty to my father goes bone deep. Until this moment, I would've sworn he wouldn't hurt a hair on my head, but the spanking doesn't worry me. In fact, I take it as a sign that I might actually get somewhere with Alex for once.

"Jealous?" Alex is breathing hard, which doesn't make sense because he's in great shape. Unless… he's as excited as I am. He yanks up my mini-skirt.

I squeal and reach back with both hands to hold it down, but he grabs my wrists and pins them behind my back. Then he lifts my skirt up to my waist and smacks my ass. I'm wearing a G-string, so his palm connects with bare skin and makes a crack that I'm sure the people in the room next door can hear. My pussy clenches at the intimacy of the act. His hand is so close to my tingling lady bits.

"Yeah, maybe." He smacks me again. "Some *stronzo* Russian tries to stop me from leaving with you? He's lucky I didn't shove his balls down his throat." He's spanking me hard, first one cheek, then the other.

I choke on my breath. I didn't expect Alex to put a claim on me. Of course, it might not mean anything. He probably thinks he owns me because he's acting as my father's agent. And Lord knows my father thinks he owns me.

He keeps spanking. "Tell me you haven't been down there every fucking night like this."

I don't answer because I'm not going to lie, and the truth is going to make him more mad. And I'm not sure I can handle more spanking, even though my pussy is wet, clit throbbing.

He takes my silence as a *yes* and spanks harder, his hand falling in swift, punctuating movements. "Tell me—" His voice goes rough, almost broken. "Tell me you didn't let those bastards take advantage of you. *Tell me!*" he roars.

Uh… what bastards?

He stops spanking me. "Jenna?" Yes, his voice sounds broken.

"No—never."

I'm still a virgin, as ridiculous as that may sound. All those years, promised to Nico Tacone—I don't know, I guess I was afraid he'd do something horrible to me if I wasn't a virgin on our wedding night. And since he set me free a few months ago, well… no one here was Alex.

So that's that.

Alex abruptly pulls me up and turns me to face him. "Never?" he croaks.

I shake my head. "Never, ever."

His mouth descends on mine in a punishing kiss.

I swoon. All this time, I've been hoping I wasn't reading an attraction that wasn't there. Praying he wouldn't reject me yet again. And now—praise the virgin *Madonna*—he's kissing me!

He palms my bare ass with both hands, squeezing and kneading the smarting flesh as his lips twist over mine, his tongue invades.

It's a wicked kiss. A demanding one.

I push my pelvis forward, stand on my tiptoes to rub higher. His cock presses into my belly with hard insistence.

Oh, God—this is it. I'm going to lose my virginity to the guy I always dreamed of giving it to.

*Alex*

I SOMEHOW FORCE myself to pull back from Jenna. She tastes like cranberry and vodka and I want to fucking devour her, but I can't.

She's the don's daughter.

Except who am I kidding? I just bent her over and spanked her ass like a naughty girl. If that's not claiming her, what is? And seriously, if I don't claim her now, the spanking would be a humiliating insult to her.

She's not tied to Nico Tacone anymore.

That means she's free.

Right?

I capture the back of her head and go in for more kissing. Her lips are soft and giving, her body molds to mine.

I don't know why, but I have to know more about the men. I'm jealous as fuck just knowing guys have seen her dressed like this.

I press her back on the bed, falling over her, still fucking her mouth with my tongue. I pin her wrists above her head and come up for air. "How many men, Jenna? Just tell me."

She frowns, her forehead wrinkling up in an adorable scowl. "I told you—none."

I can't quite breathe. "None here? Or none... ever?"

She gets smaller before my eyes and I feel like the biggest *stronzo* on Earth for diminishing her. As much as it inspires my dominant, protective instincts, I like seeing her in her sexual power. "None, ever," she mutters.

My chest tightens. *Cazzo.* Despite her oozing sexuality, Jenna Pachino is an innocent.

I kiss her again, tender this time.

And then I force myself off her. Because I'm sure as hell going to make her first time good, not some drunken hookup that she might regret tomorrow. I scoop my arms under her shoulders and knees and slide her up on the bed and under the covers.

She smiles up at me, but when I pull the covers up to her chin, she frowns. "What are you doing?"

"Putting you to bed, *tesoro mio*."

She sits up and reaches for me. "Aren't you coming?"

I step out of her reach, because, fuck, if I let her touch me, I'm going to be in that bed in a half-second. "Believe me, *bambi*, there's nothing more I want than to be pounding between those legs until you can't walk straight tomorrow, but I'm not going to." Her eyes rounded when I spoke crudely, but the way her lips part is an invitation. "I'm not going to take advantage of you when you've been drinking."

She climbs out of the bed and holds my gaze, pulling her tiny top—essentially a handkerchief held on with two threads—over her head. She isn't wearing a bra, and her breasts bounce invitingly.

Fuck. I've had a lot of women, but I've never seen a body that compares to Jenna Pachino's. But she's always done it for me, hasn't she? Of course I have to have a hard-on for the don's only daughter. I stumble back, out of reaching distance.

She climbs out of the bed and sheds the rumpled skirt next.

"Enough!" I snap when she hooks her thumbs in the waistband of her G-string. "Don't fucking cock-tease me, baby. Not when I've been shouting your name while I beat off since before you were out of your dad's house." I give my cock a hard squeeze over my pants. "Not when I'm trying to be a gentleman. You get that gorgeous ass of yours back in bed before I paint it red again."

Excitement flares in her eyes at my threat, which

comes as a relief, because I've been feeling like an asshole for taking liberties punishing her already.

She doesn't stop, though. She steps forward and loops her arms around my neck, rubbing those hard nipples against my chest.

"I mean it," I growl, but my voice comes out raspy. I grab her panties by the back string and pull up, threading them against her crack in the back, pulling taut over her clitty in the front.

Her moan nearly makes me lose it. She pants, head falling back, fingernails scoring the back of my neck.

"Aw, *bambi*, you keep making noises like that and I'm gonna end up fucking you standing. Right here, right now."

She lifts one leg, as if to line her pussy up with my throbbing dick, and I yank up on her G-string again.

"I think you need a lesson in obedience."

She pants in audible, moany little breaths.

"You gonna get in that bed—" she shakes her head as I speak, "—or do I have to spank you again?"

She nods.

*Cazzo.* Do I have the control for this?

I seriously doubt it.

To take things down a notch, I lead her over to the sofa, where I sit and pull her over my lap.

"Mmm." I swear to Christ, she starts humping it.

Jenna Pachino is fucking killing me.

She's turned the wrong way, which means I have to use my left hand to spank her. It's probably a good thing, because her ass is still pink from the slaps I laid down earlier.

"You need your ass smacked by me?" I ask. Her ass is delicious to spank—round, muscular, perfect. The perky cheeks flatten and bounce back with each slap.

"Yes," she moans.

"Say *yes, Daddy.*" I don't even know where I'm getting this shit. I'm dominant, yeah. I've always been the kinda guy who takes charge in the bedroom. I like to hold them down, even tie them up, and fuck hard.

But Jenna, she's special to me. She's the girl who offered secret smiles and stolen glances from the first day the don took me under his wing. She teased and joked with me when I was nervous, held my hand at my father's funeral, and delivered home-baked Italian dishes for the month after.

And she's hotter than sin. So yeah, I still want to dominate her, but taking good care of her is at the forefront of my mind. Which I guess translates to being her daddy.

"Yes, Daddy." She says it immediately, like there's nothing weird about me demanding she call me that. This girl was fucking made for me. I knew it.

All these years, I couldn't believe God would forsake me by handing her over to someone else.

But now she's free. The contract's been broken, Nico Tacone married his little art historian, and the mountains didn't fall. The Families didn't even squabble over it.

"Good, because I fucking love spanking you, *principessa.*"

Her ass is hot, and turning from pink to red. It strikes me with stab of horror that I might have gone too far. She is drunk, after all. She might not be experiencing the real pain of it.

I stop and rub her cheeks, handling them roughly because I can't control myself.

She rolls her hips, taunting me. Teasing me. Offering herself to me.

Not. Tonight.

*Cazzo.*

I bring two fingers between her legs. Her panties are soaked. I slip under them and work her clit, rubbing it lightly at first, then penetrating her with just one finger. She's tight—but I work my digit in, then add a second one.

Her juices leak freely, her moans sound wanton. "Alex," she breathes.

I pull my fingers out and smack her ass. "*Daddy.*"

"Daddy," she repeats immediately.

"Good girl." I reward her with a firmer treatment of her clit, circling it, rubbing. I penetrate her again with two fingers, pumping them in and out.

"Alex-Daddy-please," she begs, stringing the words together.

"You need to come already, baby?"

"Yes, please. Oh!"

I love the way she arches her back like a little kitten, sticking her ass up in the air to meet my fingers. I fuck her faster with them, harder. I insinuate my thumb between her ass cheeks and press it against her anus.

She comes immediately, her muscles spasming around my fingers, her body flattening and going rigid. She kicks her legs out straight behind her, tightening all the muscles as her pussy squeezes and releases.

"That's it, *principessa*," I murmur. When she's done, I

slip my fingers out and drop a kiss on her reddened cheeks. "Now, get in bed." I help her to her feet. I can't fucking stand, because my boner is so hard against my leg I'm afraid it will break off.

"What about you?" She looks down at my obvious discomfort.

I wave an impatient hand. "Get in the fucking bed, little girl. Your ass is red enough."

She smiles and cups her ass, then shrugs and heads to the bathroom to brush her teeth.

She must be sobering up.

And *no*, I tell myself firmly, that doesn't mean I can fuck her now.

# CHAPTER 2

I WAKE in the morning with a headache and a case of cottonmouth. A familiar, manly scent fills my nostrils and I sit bolt upright with a gasp.

It definitely wasn't a dream.

Alex sits on the hotel suite sofa, reading a newspaper, still dressed in his fine Italian suit like he never slept. There's a coffee carafe and a tray of food from room service on the table, though. How did I sleep through all that?

"*Buongiorno.*" Alex's deep raspy voice goes straight to my lady parts.

And that's when I realize I'm naked except for my G-string. I yank the sheet up to my shoulders, then climb

15

out, keeping it intact. I have to tug a couple of times to pull it off the bed.

Alex watches all this with a mixture of amusement and the smoldering desire I remember always burned in his eyes for me.

Oh, God—it's really true! It's really happening. Alex is here, in my suite, and he's into me. So into me, he pleasured me last night without taking any satisfaction of his own.

*There's nothing more I want than to be pounding between those legs until you can't walk straight tomorrow.*

"*Buongiorno.* I, um, am just going to brush my teeth."

The corners of Alex's lips turn up. "You do that. I put a bottle of ibuprofen out on the counter in case you need it."

My heart somersaults. "You did?" Sweet man.

*Don't read too much into it*, I caution myself. Alex is a player. If he's into me, it's only because I'm no longer off limits. He needs to check me off his list. Or make me a notch in his bedpost—whatever the saying is.

I pop a couple of the painkillers, brush my teeth, and wash my face. Then I drop the sheet, turn around, and look at my ass in the mirror. There are a couple of small red marks, but otherwise, nothing. I squeeze my cheeks with my hands. No residual pain at all. Which seems amazing because I remember him spanking me pretty hard.

And the memory makes my nipples pebble up and my pussy clench.

I left the door ajar and suddenly Alex is there, standing in front of me, taking in the whole scene.

My face grows hot, but Alex steps right into the bathroom with me. "Let me have a look." He turns me around and bends me over the bathroom counter. "I left marks." He sounds stricken. He rubs my ass in a slow, circular motion. "Does it hurt, *bambi?*"

"No." I'm breathless.

"Are you sure? I didn't mean to hurt you."

Well, this is my chance. He may be a player, but I need to get my V-card checked by someone, and he's the guy I always dreamed of doing it. I turn around and place my hands on his chest. "Really? Because it sure felt like you did."

He smirks and grabs my ass with both of his large palms. "Well, a little punishment was in order."

"Because I was so bad?" I purr.

"Yes." He squeezes my cheeks.

"Is that why you're here? To punish me?" I know it's not why, but I like that idea far more than what his presence really means. He's here to drag me home.

And I sure as hell don't want to go back. I've had enough of living my life for my parents. It's time for me to start making choices for myself.

His eyes are so dark, they're black. He cups my chin in that dominant, take-charge way he has. "I didn't know you'd still be so sassy once you sobered up."

I lift my chin. "You don't know a lot of things about me."

His expression darkens. "No, but I intend to find out." He sounds threatening, and a shiver runs down my spine. I don't know exactly what he does in the family business, just like I don't know what my dad does. The women of

17

the family make it their business to never know. It's one part safety, one part sanity-keeping measures. Because if we knew, would we really stick around?

And that's another reason why I like the idea of staying gone.

I ran away from that life, the misery my father wanted to twist me into. I don't need Alex dragging me back, no matter how persuasive or beautiful he may be.

I pull back out of his grip and put my hands on my hips. It's hard to muster bravado in nothing but a G-string but I do my best. "I'm not going back, Alex."

He studies my face, nothing showing in his expression. Then he tilts his head to the side. "I'm not leaving without you."

And just like that, my nipples bead up, as if he just declared we'd be having sex soon.

He doesn't miss it, his gaze dropping to my breasts and growing hungry.

"I-I guess we're at a standoff, then."

He takes a step forward, dark and dangerous. "I guess we are." He takes another step and his hand tangles in the back of my hair. "Good. That gives me time to punish you thoroughly."

My knees go weak and his fist tightens at my scalp, tugging my head back.

"Wh-what for?" My heart's beating so hard, I'm sure he can see it under my skin.

He brushes his lips over mine, then nips my lower lip, holding it a moment between his teeth. It's a slow release, my plump flesh dragging under his bite until it releases with a pop. "For running away, *tesoro mio.* You worried your father to death."

*My father.*

Just like that, my excitement fizzles.

Alex is here on a job. My father sent him. He may be showing more interest in me than usual, but that's just his usual playboy persona. He held it back from me before, because I was off-limits.

So yeah. If I decide to let him check off my V-card, that's one thing. But this man is not here for me. He's a player and he's on a job. So if I want to play, too, that's fine. But I'd better guard the hell out of my heart.

*Alex*

JENNA'S smile crashes when I mention her father, and I quickly try to remedy the mistake. "I was worried about you."

But it's too late—the moment is gone. Jenna backs away from me, out of the bathroom, and she hurries to get dressed.

I somehow resurrect the gentleman in me and turn my back to give her privacy.

It's probably just as well she retreated. I shouldn't be getting involved with the mafia princess. Just because Don Giuseppe sent me here to get her doesn't mean he gave me permission to claim her. In fact, for all I know, he might take my interest in his daughter as a supreme disrespect and put a bullet through my head.

I don't think so—the old man loves me like a son—but you never know.

So I'll just have a conversation with Jenna about last night being a mistake and we'll keep it our secret. But my resolve vanishes when I turn and find her dressed in shorts that cover less than a pair of panties, and her bikini top.

In fact, I choke on my own spit.

"What the fuck are you wearing?"

Her smile is all cock-tease—the same one she used as a drop-dead gorgeous eighteen-year-old when she'd saunter past me to the pool in nothing but a string bikini.

"You're doing that on purpose," I growl. My balls are already blue from last night and our little scene in the bathroom. Now, need turns me rough. She grabs a piece of fruit from the plate I ordered in, takes her keycard from the table, and walks out the door.

Growling, I yank off my tie, toss it over the sofa arm, and follow her out.

She sashays ahead of me, swinging her hips more than should be legal. I raise my eyes heavenward.

"Jenna, where are you going?"

She tosses her chestnut-brown hair over her shoulder when she looks at me. "For my morning walk on the beach." Her eyes drop to my polished dress shoes. "You're going to have a hard time in those." She keeps walking, shaking that ass.

I sigh and push my hand through my hair. What am I

even doing? I came here to bring her home. Antagonizing her wasn't my goal. "Wait—Jenna."

She must hear the change of my tone from bossy to sincere, because she stops and turns, cocking a hip. "Yes?" She's enjoying herself immensely.

"Do you *want* me to come?"

Her smile wobbles, the confident facade falls away. Now she's being real, too. "Um, yeah. I guess so."

The glimmer of her vulnerability makes my chest squeeze. "Come here." I hold out my hand.

She loses the swagger when she comes back to me and places her hand in mine so easily. So trusting. Just like last night when she told that asshole Russian I was hers. Damn straight, I'm hers. I'm glad she knows it.

"Let me get changed, okay?"

The way she looks up at me with those long-lashed hazel eyes makes the floor tilt. "Sure."

We head to the room I booked in the same hotel. "I'm going to have to go shopping for beach clothes," I admit. I brought swim trunks, but that's about it. My Chicago wardrobe doesn't have much Tommy Bahama.

"I'll go shopping with you," Jenna pipes up.

I chuckle at her enthusiasm. She got her degree in fashion merchandising and her father always complains about how much she and her mother shop. "Are you going to be my personal stylist?" I take off my button-down and pull off the undershirt. I might as well get a tan while I'm here.

"Definitely." There's a twinkle in her eye and I enjoy the way she watches me, like she's drinking in the sight of my bare chest and tattooed arms.

"Like what you see?" I wink.

She smiles, but blushes.

I look right at her while I change into the swim trunks, daring her to keep watching. My cock is still thick for her —it's a twenty-four/seven problem when she's around. It salutes her when it pops out of my boxer briefs.

A stain of pink colors her cheeks, and she drags her lower lip between her teeth, eyes glued to my member. I pull on the swim trunks.

She keeps watching.

I gotta get out of this room before I lose control. I grab my keycard, shove it in the Velcro pocket of the swim trunks, and hold out my hand. "Let's go, *bambi*. Before you get yourself into more trouble than you can handle looking at me that way."

I go barefooted, which sucks until we reach the soft sand of the beach. "I'm buying flip-flops first thing," I declare as my toes sink into the white sand.

"We'll find you everything you need." I like the confidence in Jenna's tone. Like this is her job and she knows how to do it. I think her father always thought it was a shit degree, but he didn't care. Everyone knew college was just time to stall Jenna's arranged marriage to Nico Tacone.

"You really enjoy shopping for other people?"

"Yes!" She smiles up at me. "I can make anyone look good. Any size or shape. It's all about waist placement and body shape. Dressing with the right layers and lines for the body."

I'm an idiot for not knowing there'd be science behind fashion design or styling.

"Oh, yeah? I'd love to watch you work, sometime."

Her step falters and she peers up at me, shading her eyes from the sun. "Are you making fun of me?"

"Fuck, no! Why would you say that?"

"I know my dad thinks I wasted my education."

"Who gives a shit what your dad thinks?" I say it automatically, before I even realize how blasphemous it is to say about the don, the man I owe everything to.

Her eyes widen and that's my clue I disrespected him.

"I mean, don't tell him I said that, but *bambi*, if you've found what you love to do, and you're good at it—well, that's a gift. Most people spend their whole lives looking."

"You really think so?" Her hand tightens in mine.

"Yes."

"Because I have this idea." The words come out rushed, and her face lights up in a way that makes me want to kiss her. "It would be online styling. They send me photos showing me their shape and taste and I put together a buy list. Like ten to twelve items. Everything that's in style, custom picked to their body shape, personal style, and budget. I could get high-fashion labels for the movie stars, or fashionistas, and off-brand stuff for those people who don't have money to waste."

"And they'd pay you a flat fee?"

"Yes, but also I could work out a commission from the stores, you know? So I get money on both ends. And as I grew the business, I'd add stylists. Train them in my method and have people under me..." She stops speaking and adjusts the straps of her bikini top, like she's suddenly self-conscious. "I don't know, it's just an idea. But it's something I could do from anywhere, you know? Even here."

I stop and tug her around to face me. "You're thinking about staying here?"

She doesn't quite meet my eyes. Probably because she knows there's no chance in hell I'm not going to bring her home. Even if she runs again, I will track her down and follow her. The only reason I wasn't here months ago was because Don Giuseppe had word the Tacones had bankrolled her disappearance, and she was safe.

"I'm not going home, Alex." Her hazel eyes are wide and serious.

"There's nothing to run from anymore. Surely you know the marriage contract is off? Nico Tacone married a girl last week. You're free now, Jenna."

Something flickers in Jenna's face. *Pain.* The deal may be off, but the wound her father inflicted is still there. Well, I don't blame her for being bitter.

I frown and pick up her hand again, tug her toward the ocean. "Come on, I'll race you to the water."

She only hesitates a half-beat before she takes off, her long legs streaking for the waves. I give her a head start, then follow, catching her when she's ankle deep in the ocean and spinning her around.

# CHAPTER 3

 enna

ALEX DESERVES A MEDAL. He's shown endless patience playing fashion model to me all afternoon and into the evening—trying on endless combinations of clothing, shoes, sunglasses until I'm satisfied he's the best-dressed man on the island.

When we go to pay for it, I pull out the credit card Nico Tacone set me up with, but Alex snatches it out of my hand and folds it in half until it breaks. He tosses his own card on the counter.

I can't say I'm surprised, but I feel like a naughty coed losing her credit card privileges. Which reminds me of Alex's little quirk last night. I turn on my best sex kitten voice and wiggle a finger through the buttonhole on his new shirt. "Is Daddy taking away my allowance?"

He grabs my wrist, eyes going dark with lust.

The salesgirl smirks as she rings up the mountain of clothes I picked out for him.

He pulls my fingers to his mouth and bites my knuckle, then kisses it. His lips are impossibly soft for such a manly man. "I'm gonna do more than that to you, *piccolina.*"

I press my body up against his. "Oh, yeah?" I purr.

"Believe it," he whispers.

A shiver runs up my spine and a slow pulse starts between my legs.

By the time we pay for the clothing and catch a cab back to the hotel, I'm horny as hell. Alex walks me straight to my suite. I'm thinking he's just dropping me off, but he comes in.

"Don't you want to bring those clothes back to your place?"

He shakes his head. "I'm moving in here. Somebody needs to keep an eye on you, and that somebody is me."

I twirl a lock of hair, playing coquette. "Because I'm so bad?"

His lips twitch. "That's right." His voice is deeper than usual. His presence fills the suite, overpowers me.

"Are you going to spank me again?" My heart races at my daring.

He purses his lips like he's considering, then nods slowly. "I'm going to spank your ass every night until you agree to come home with me."

My stomach knots just a bit at the *home with me* part.

Because I wish he meant it literally, but he doesn't. He means home to my father. This is a duty for him. But one he happens to be enjoying at the moment. And I intend to enjoy it with him.

"You think that will change my mind?" I pivot my hips right and left like I'm swishing a skirt.

He gives a nonchalant shrug. "Eventually, I'll bring you to heel."

My pussy clenches at the idea of his taking me in hand.

He crooks a finger. "You're just begging for that spanking right now, aren't you, *cara?*"

When I don't move, he snatches my wrist and pulls me up against his hard body. "Come here, baby. You've been teasing me with that ass all day long. It's time for payback."

I swoon a little. I freakin' love when he talks tough with me. I'm wearing a pair of skin-tight white capri jeans and he unbuttons them.

My legs tremble as he pulls them down over my ass, all the way to my ankles. He crouches at my feet, infinitely gentle as he tugs them off one foot and then the other.

"And now for these." He peels down my lace panties.

I suck in a breath. I shaved myself bare for him when I took a shower before we went shopping.

He's not disappointed. "Oh, baby. Oh, fuck, baby. Look at that pussy." He brushes my nether lips with his thumb, then curls my toes when he drags his tongue in a long line up the seam. "Did you do this for me, *amore?*"

"Um…" I can't speak because he's applying his tongue to my clit.

He pulls back, eyes blazing. "Don't tell me you keep this pussy shaved on the regular."

I step back, because he's being a prick. "Why not?"

He stands up, still frowning. He pulls my blouse off over my head. "Because I can't fucking stand knowing this sexy pussy was right there. Every fucking time I talked to you. Every time another guy talked to you." His voice is rough.

I give a shaky laugh. "You're nuts, Alessandro, you know that?" I reach up and pull his head down for a kiss.

He claims my mouth with bruising force, at the same time he unhooks my bra in the back and pulls it off my shoulders.

It's just like last night—I'm naked, he's fully dressed.

"Come here, sweetheart." He pulls me to the couch again, and across his knees. I'm creaming so hard for him, I'll probably wet his trousers. Memories of the way he brought me to orgasm last night stoke the flames that are already smoldering for him.

"Yeah, I'm going to be spanking this ass nightly," he mutters just before his hand crashes down right in the center of my ass.

I yelp. "Are you going to spank that hard?"

He chuckles. "Depends, *bambina*. Are you going to be a good girl for Daddy?"

I moan and roll my hips on his lap. He slaps me again and I yelp. "Yes, Daddy."

"That's what I want to hear." But he starts up a rhythm, spanking me much harder than I think he should for a little slap and tickle before sex.

"Ouch, ouch, ouch," I complain, reaching back to cover. "Am I really in trouble?"

"Oh, you're in worlds of trouble, *amore*. Worlds."

"Why—ouch! Alex!"

He stops and rubs his large palm in a circle over my smarting ass, soothing away the sting. "For starters"—he slaps me again—"you've made me suffer all these years. You enjoyed my fucking suffering. Every time you pranced by me at your father's house wearing something highly inappropriate." He gives me three hard slaps. My whole ass twitches and tingles now, heat settling in.

"It's not my fault you came by when I was still in my jammies," I choke, remembering a time when his eyes nearly bugged out at seeing me in a cami top and short shorts.

"Those were not jammies!" Clearly he remembers the same scene. And clearly it still bothers him because his hand crashes down so hard I lose my breath. Each spank jiggles my lady bits, making them swell between my legs.

"Alex—ouch! Please!"

"I'm not stopping this spanking until you apologize." He's still spanking fast and hard and I'm losing the fun of it now.

"I'm sorry!" I holler.

"I'm sorry I was a cock-tease, Daddy," he prompts.

"I'm sorry I was a cock-tease, Daddy!" I shout back.

He stops spanking and rubs.

Endorphins must be kicking in, because the pain has changed. It's just a pulsing, heat and the throb of my clit, needy and swollen between my legs.

"Good girl." Alex strokes me with both hands, one

running up and down my back while the other circles my ass. "You took your spanking so well, *cara mia.*"

"You were mean," I sulk, because—yeah. It was definitely more than I bargained for. I guess if he spanked me that hard last night, I didn't notice because I was drunk.

"I know, baby, but Daddy's going to reward his princess, too." He pulls me up and arranges me on his lap, my back facing his front. He drapes my knees on the outside of his, spreading me wide. "Does this pretty pussy need some attention from Daddy now?"

"Y-yes," I breathe as he taps my clit.

He gives it a light slap and I jerk in surprise. It didn't hurt, but I never knew it was a thing. "Put your hands behind your head, baby girl."

My movements stutter on the way to obey him, not quite sure what he wants, but then I understand. The position lifts and separates my breasts, which he now reaches around to squeeze and cup. He tugs my nipples, pinches them, rolls them between his fingers. I wriggle on his lap, wanting the attention to return south.

It does, shortly.

"Now, leave your hands there, *piccolina.* I'm going to spank your pussy. Do you think you can come from nothing more than a pussy spanking?" He gives my lady parts a sharp tap.

"I-I don't know." Until a moment ago, I didn't even know what a pussy spanking was. I'm one part scared, two parts excited.

"Let's find out." He slaps again and again—not hard, but firm. Pleasure blooms, hot and furious, heat gathering and pulsing. He picks up his speed, lightening the spanks so they're quick *tap-tap-taps.*

I throw my head back over his shoulder, moaning for release. I want to move my hands, but I don't want to disobey him.

"Alex," I pant. *"Alex."*

He understands me, slapping even faster.

I climax. My hands fly off my head, searching for his and when I find it, I tear at his hair. He keeps up his quick taps, as I plunge into ecstasy, my body releasing in a shock of heat and tingles.

"That's it, baby," Alex murmurs in my ear.

I'm still in outer space, rocketing around the moon, but his lips against my skin bring me back, ground me.

"Alex."

"Say *thank you, Daddy.*" He screws one finger into my tight channel and I gasp and push against it.

"Thank you, Daddy."

*Alex*

DAMN, pleasuring Jenna is off the charts exciting. I've had a lot of women, but I've never been so satisfied by making one come before. Even with my dick this hard.

I don't give her much of a break between her first orgasm and working on building to a second one. I get two fingers inside her and she starts riding them like the most erotic cowgirl I've ever seen.

It's too much—I'm getting lightheaded from need.

"You know what happens when you're naughty, baby?" I wiggle my fingers inside her but I can't quite reach her G-spot.

"What?" she breathes.

"You take your daddy's big cock. Are you ready for it?"

"Yes." She rocks over my fingers.

"Yes, Daddy," I correct her. I don't know why I'm getting into being her daddy so much, but I am.

"Yes, Daddy."

"Good." I help her up and arrange her on her hands and knees in the middle of the bed. Then I push her torso down and bind her wrists behind her back with the tie I left in here this morning. Only then do I realize I picked quite a position for her first time. Maybe not my best choice. I go for a bit of explanation. "This is a good angle for me to get in deep, baby. Hit your G-spot and make you scream. But if you're scared or uncomfortable, tell me."

"I'm never scared with you."

She answers so immediately, it must be true. I'm humbled. In awe of her, really. How could anyone surrender control so completely, with so much trust? And to me?

It's a fucking gift.

"I'm going to use plenty of lube, *cara*, so it shouldn't hurt. You tell me if it does." I went down to the convenience store last night after she fell asleep and bought lubricant and extra lubed condoms for her deflowering. I guess I knew we'd end up here, despite my better intentions.

I shove down my shorts and give my cock a hard yank. My thighs are already shaking with need. I'm not going to last long in her. I snap open the foil and roll on the lubed condom, add more lube, then I rub the head over her dewy opening.

She arches and pushes back.

"Think you can take me?" I say it like a dare, and she pushes back more, takes the head.

She groans.

"I know, *amore*. You're so fucking tight. Do you have any idea what your tight little pussy is doing to me right now?"

She moans again, more wanton this time.

I ease forward. "Be a good girl and take every inch of Daddy's cock. Tell me you want it."

"I want it," she pants.

I never get the sensation of tearing through a barrier, but I go slowly, giving her time to get used to my size. When I'm fully seated, I only ease out an inch and push back in.

"Ohhhhh," Jenna groans.

"You okay?"

"Yes. Yes, yes, yes. Go on."

Sweat gathers at my hairline from the strain of holding back. Every muscle in my back and shoulders is cranked tight. My ass, my thighs, even my fucking feet shake from the effort. I grip her hips and give her a little more slide, bumping her ass on my instrokes.

"Oh! Yes! Oh, wow."

"You're Daddy's little fuck-toy right now, aren't you?

Looking sweet, all tied up with a bow. This is how I've always wanted you."

Okay, I can't believe I just admitted that to her. I am a filthy bastard, but she doesn't seem to mind. She croons encouragingly.

"You like being filled by Daddy's big cock?"

"Yes, Daddy!" she cries.

I'm lost. My fingers dig into her flesh as I bang her harder, my loins slapping against her pink ass, my cock plunging deep enough to hit her inner wall. "*Cazzo, cazzo!*" I curse, control gone. I fuck her hard, harder than I should, but I can't pull back. I need her too badly.

She's crying out with each breath, porn star noises, and I'm beyond saving.

I roar as cum shoots down my length. I push forward, forcing her flat on her belly as I release, then I fuck her some more in the new position, just because it feels too damn good to stop. Her pussy squeezes me in tight little pulses as she reaches orgasm with me.

Finally, the rush eases and my brain returns. I quickly untie her wrists before I cause her real discomfort and I cover her body with my own. My lips brush her neck, her jaw, her ear.

"*Bambina*, you have a magic pussy. Best fucking pussy I've ever had in my life. I swear to *la Madonna*."

She gives a broken laugh.

I roll her to her back to make sure she's okay. Her face is flushed, eyes still glazed. A beautiful smile plays over her lush lips. I kiss down her torso, starting with her collarbone, between her breasts, her soft belly, the apex of her shaved pussy.

"This pussy belongs to me." I can no longer withhold my claim—especially not now that I've had her. I pull one of her knees open and just stare down at it. "I can't fucking stand that Nico Tacone had a claim on you all these years."

"Alex." I hear the censure in her voice as she pushes herself up on her forearms.

"I'm sorry. I know it wasn't your fault. It wasn't even his. But it makes me fucking crazy." I pick up both her ankles and lift them in the air, exposing her bare ass and I start spanking again, hard and fast. "This ass belongs to me."

"Okay, Alex! Enough!" She kicks hard enough to get one ankle free and I give my head a shake. I know I've gone way too far. I have no right to lay claim to Jenna Pachino. Hell, if I wanted to keep my balls, I wouldn't have even touched her. But the alpha male in me can't stop. Not until she's mine.

I reclaim her ankle but don't spank her again. I just rub her ass, let my thumb trail between her cheeks to find the pucker of her anus. "I know I'm a dick," I admit. "I can't own you, can I, baby? You're an independent young woman. You have a bright career mapped out for yourself. No way you wanna get chained to *Cosa Nostra*. Not after you barely escaped it."

She blinks at me, lashes wet.

I lower her legs and ease her to her side, then settle in behind her, one arm draped over her waist. "My ma couldn't handle it." I can't believe I'm talking about it. I've never talked about it. But Jenna brings all this out in me.

"That's why she left us. I was only seven when she walked out on my dad and my brother and me."

Jenna goes still, then rolls over to face me. Her brows go down, a line of concern between them.

"Because of *La Famiglia?*"

"*Sì*. My dad said it was too much to take, the worry and guilt. She was a sensitive soul. She didn't care about the money, just fell in love with my dad. Maybe she loved him too much. I remember she used to wring her hands and pace around every night he was out. She'd rush to the door when he got back and throw her arms around his neck saying *thank God you're home.*"

Jenna's eyes fill with tears. "I understand how she feels."

I stroke her cheek with my thumb. "Do you worry, too, baby?"

She nods. "I tried to follow my mom's lead. Pretend there's nothing different about our family. Stick my head in the sand. But how could I when we went to funeral after funeral? When every guy was either in jail or dead? And all that time I had the marriage contract hanging over my head."

I wrap her up in my arms. "I know, baby. That was bullshit. I'm so sorry." I kiss her hair, which is silky soft. "You were so brave."

"And my mom?" she croaks. "How could she let it happen?"

I shake my head. "I don't know, *bambi.*"

"How could you?" she whispers. Tears drip down her cheeks.

There it is. The accusation I've been hurling at myself

36

all these years. How could I let such a thing happen to a sweet, innocent girl? *Grazie a Dio* it didn't actually manifest, but what if it had? I have no answer for her.

My stomach churns. I push up to sit.

She also sits up, wrapping her arms around her waist. "Did you even stick up for me? Did he ever talk about it?"

I get up off the bed to pace. "Yes, I fucking advocated for you!" I thunder, although I don't know why I'm raising my voice to her. It's her father I'm really angry at. "The second he got that letter from you, I told him it was time to renegotiate. That the contract was too old-fashioned to enforce in this day and age. Tacone's rich, though, so he wanted to figure out a way to keep him on the hook, but I talked him out all of it. And no blame was put on you. When you go home, you'll be welcomed with open arms. I promise you that, or I wouldn't have come for you."

"I'm not going home," she says through stiff lips.

For the first time, I realize I may not be doing her a favor by bringing her back. All this time, I was thinking I was doing the right thing. It was time to bring the lost little lamb home. But Jenna's not lost. She's a smart woman with big ideas who deserves a future much brighter than the one her father originally chose for her. And if I'm crushing even one iota of her new persona, then I deserve to rot in hell.

But she can't live on Nico Tacone's dime forever, either. And I can't pretend I didn't find her. Or that she ran away again. Don G wouldn't tolerate that kind of sloppiness.

I sink onto the sofa and drop my head into my hands.

What in the fuck am I going to do?

~

*Jenna*

I SHOULDN'T HAVE LASHED out at Alex. It wasn't his fault. And for me to pretend he'd be able to make my father do anything is ludicrous. My father rules with an iron fist.

He looks so torn up now, I feel bad. I get up from the bed and pull on a sundress, then I walk over to him. When he lifts his head from his hands, I plop onto his lap.

Surprise flickers over his face, but his arms instantly come around me, cradling me, just like I wanted to be held.

"I don't blame you," I say softly. "You had nothing to do with it. I'm sorry."

"No, don't be sorry, angel. You're right to be mad. The whole family hung you out to dry. It was unbelievably fucked up."

I kiss his stubbled jaw and he turns into it, captures my jaw with his hand and kisses me in that dominating way of his, tongue sweeping between my lips, mouth twisting over mine. I grow breathless, and he breaks the kiss with a curse.

"*Cazzo*, I need to fuck you again. Let's get out of this suite, baby, before I forget to be gentle with you."

I love that he wants to be gentle and I also love that he loses control. Yeah, I'm a bit sore between my legs now, but the way he claimed me was perfect. So rough, so virile. So demanding. I love that he put me on my knees and tied me up.

Honestly, for me, it was so much better than some gentle 'first time' screw missionary style. I would've felt awkward and not known what to do. As it was, he removed all need for me to know out of my hands. He took charge and brought me more pleasure than I imagined possible. I'm glad I waited and I'm glad he's the one who deflowered me.

"How about some dinner?" He lifts me off his lap and his eyes sweep over the sundress, which gathers between my breasts and ties behind my neck. His jaw tightens. "Just put on some panties, for fuck's sake," he snaps, like I'm already testing his resolve not to throw me down and take me again.

"Yes, Daddy," I say brightly, earning a reluctant smile.

I slip on a G-string that won't show under the dress and take his hand. He leads me out to the hallway, where he stops and kisses me again—a full kiss, arm around my waist, lips tormenting mine.

"You look at any other man tonight, I'm going to take you back here and whip your ass with my belt," he says. There's a teasing quality to his voice that lets me know he doesn't mean it, although sometimes I'm not really sure. I think he could be that possessive.

But no. A player like Alex wouldn't really be possessive of me.

Would he?

# CHAPTER 4

lex

"So tell me all the things you need to start your business." I have the hotel pad of paper and pen in my hands. We're still in bed. By some miracle, I managed not to hold Jenna down and claim her hard last night, but this morning she wasn't so lucky.

Or maybe it was lucky, considering she probably woke up the entire hotel with her screams. I'd be buffing my nails over my prowess if I wasn't so enthralled with just being with Jenna. Just hanging out in bed together.

Believe me, in my long history of taking women home and fucking them thoroughly, I never played cuddle me afterward.

But we're propped up naked in the sheets, just talking.

Just fucking talking about everything under the sun, and I've never felt more like myself.

Jenna lights up, the way she did yesterday talking about her business concept. "Well, that's the beauty of it. I don't need anything but a computer and internet connection. I don't have to carry any inventory or purchase any equipment. I don't need my own building or storefront. It's simple."

I nod and write 'computer' on the list. "Do you already have a computer?"

"Well, sure. I have my old laptop from college." She waves at the desk, where a MacBook is plugged in.

"Do you like that one? Do you need something faster? Better? Newer?"

Her eyes narrow, lips purse into a sexy smile. "Why, Daddy?" She crawls over me and straddles my lap. "Are you going to give me an allowance?"

I groan as my cock returns to insta-stiff and adjust her hips so her pussy rubs right over it. "Yes, but there are certain duties you'll be expected to complete," I manage to choke as she rocks her pelvis and grinds over me.

She's watching my face, clearly enjoying the power she holds over me now. She lifts her hips and I reach to yank her back, but she crawls lower. "Is this one of them?" She licks her lips, fisting my cock in one hand.

I can't stop the growl that rockets from my throat. "*Cazzo, bambina. Cazzo.*"

She plays innocent coquette. "You need me here?" She lowers her moistened lips to the head and lays one soft kiss on the underside.

"Don't tease, baby. You don't want to find out what happens when you tease."

She raises her brows with exaggerated innocence. "No?"

I arch a stern brow. "You wanna find yourself on your back with my cock so far down your throat you can't scream for mercy?"

She chokes on a giggle. "No, Daddy." She takes me into her mouth. I can't decide if I'm pissed or thrilled to see that it's not her first time giving head. She definitely knows her way around a cock. But most good Catholic girls do. It must be part of the training from the nuns. Heh.

Yeah, forgive me, Father for I have sinned. *Oh, Christ!*

She sucks me deep and my balls draw up tight. Her tongue swishes on the underside of my length as she pulls back, drawing hard enough to pull the chrome off a bumper.

I practically whimper. Me, a fucking soldier. That's what she does to me. Nothing's hotter than Jenna Pachino with her lips around my cock. I'm not kidding.

Those big hazel eyes watch my face, judging my pleasure.

"Baby, I'm gonna double your allowance." I thrust my hips up, fucking her mouth.

She pops off and laughs, a husky sound that only fuels my hunger. "Oh, yeah?" She takes my cock between her tits and shoves them together, titty fucking me. Or am I titty fucking her? Who gives a shit—it's hot. "What are my other duties?" She puts her tongue out so the head of my cock hits it when it reaches the top of her tit-tunnel.

My eyes roll back in my head. "Jesus, Jenna. Fuck. This is your number one duty. *Capiche?* I want my cock sucked like this every fucking morning until the day I die." I thrust my hips wildly, which only succeeds in dislodging it from her breasts. "That's not too much to ask, is it?"

"Hmm. It might be. Depends on the allowance." She takes me in her mouth again, lowering until the head of my cock hits the pocket of her cheek.

"Oh, I'll make it good, *piccolina.* I'll make you scream all night long."

She gets excited, bobbing up and down over my cock faster, sticking her ass out and waggling it as she goes.

"Goddamn. You're like a fucking sex goddess. A sex kitten. I gotta get you a pair of ears and a tail."

She pops off again and crawls up me, lines her pussy up with my cock. There's a flicker of uncertainty, but I hate to take over when she's obviously having fun exploring her power.

"There's a condom on the table there." I lift my chin to the bedside table. She picks up the box and fumbles with it.

"I'll do it, angel." I take one out, snap it open, and roll it on in record time. Her blush reminds me to dial back my mounting aggression. I'm the kinda guy who needs to be in charge at all times, but I'm gonna let her stay on top, let her explore.

She climbs on and rubs my cock over her entrance, then lifts up and takes me deep.

I hold her hips and thrust up, forgetting to let her lead. "That's good, baby. That's so good. This is your second duty. And there'll be others. A whole lot of others." I'm controlling her completely, pulling her over my cock as I thrust up to meet her with each glide. Her tits bounce with each thrust, her hair shakes and swings.

"Like what?" She sounds breathless.

"All kinds of things. Anything Daddy orders you to do. If I say text me a picture of your breasts, you take the fucking pic. If I tell you to take off your clothes and wait on your knees for me when I get home, I'd better find you that way."

"Or else you'll spank me?" She's rocking hard now, making little cries as she pants.

"I'll punish you, *bambi*. Turn your naughty ass red. Stand you in the corner. Fuck your ass with my big cock."

She comes—I swear to Christ. I thought I'd come first, but the dirty talk sends her over the edge. She truly is my perfect match.

I grab her hips and pump hard into her a few times until I come, too.

Satisfaction.

I've never known this level of pleasure was even possible. Not just physical pleasure, but emotional. The whole thing. I'm happy. Comfortable. Sexed out of my mind.

I definitely don't want to think about anything beyond this hotel suite. Not about Don G or Chicago. Not about convincing Jenna to come back. Or whether I'll be able to keep her when we get home.

*Jenna*

I TRY to get up and get dressed, but Alex won't let me.

"No, *bambi*. You have homework to do." He turns me around and pushes me down in the chair at the desk.

"What homework?"

I'm totally naked, so it feels awkward, at best.

He wraps his tie around my waist, securing me to the chair. It's symbolic, of course, because all I have to do is pull the end of the bow and I'm free, but there's something so sexy about being bound by him.

He drops a notepad and pen in front of me. "You can't get up until you've made a list of all the steps that need to happen for you to get your business up and running."

I stare up at him in surprise.

He smiles down at me. Lord, he looks like a Greek god. His dark thick lashes curl above chocolate brown eyes. The stubble on his square jaw gives him a rough, sexy look. And more than that, warmth and affection shines in his eyes. I've never seen his expression so soft and open.

But maybe this is just how people look after great sex. I shouldn't read too much into it.

He taps the notebook. "I'm setting a timer. Thirty minutes to brainstorm. If this notepad isn't full of ideas by the time my alarm goes off, you're going over the desk for a spanking. *Capiche?*"

I smile, wings flapping in my chest. "Yes, Daddy."

He touches my nose. "Good girl."

I have a hard time not watching him move around the suite, getting dressed, but when he sends me a stern look, my pussy clenches and I look back to the paper.

Okay, the steps to getting my business up and running. Great question.

I start the list. Make a website, contact merchandisers for discounts, advertise. Where to advertise? Facebook. Instagram. My Pinterest page has a million followers, so that's a great place. What else? Develop a pricing structure. Get some media coverage in national magazines. That's gonna be hard, but I believe anything's possible. I've made dream boards before. I had Ibiza on one and now I'm here.

Before I know it, the timer goes off.

"Let's see how you did." Alex stands behind me, freshly showered and fully dressed. I think he loves the power position it puts him in to have me naked and him clothed. Or maybe it's me who loves it. He reaches over my shoulder and flips the pages. "You filled the whole pad. Good work, angel." He kisses my temple and unties me from the chair. "I guess I'll let you up."

I stand and face him, my hands on his well-built chest. "Thanks," I murmur, lifting my face for a kiss.

He dips in for a taste. "For what?"

"For making me do that. For believing in my dream. I —" I stop, suddenly overwhelmed with emotion. His face grows serious watching me. "No one ever takes me seriously. It means so much to me that you do."

"It's not a dream," he says firmly, taking me aback. "It's a plan. A really good plan. I'm ready to invest if you need investors. Anything you need, baby. I'm your man."

It's a little hard to stand up because my legs get wobbly for a second. I pull his mouth down to mine and show my appreciation until his cock gets hard against my belly and he pushes me away with a curse.

"I could stay in here and fuck you all day, baby. But I have an island to see. Wanna show me around?"

The wings take off soaring again. "Yeah," I say, breathless with joy. "Let me take a quick shower."

# CHAPTER 5

Don Giuseppe calls during dinner. We're sitting at an outdoor restaurant on the beach, indulging in fresh fish and rice after our day out sightseeing. Anybody else I would left swipe. For sure.

But he's the fucking don.

"*Scusa,*" I murmur to Jenna, standing up.

Her eyes go wide and follow me as I walk down to the beach. I'm sure she knows who it is.

I clear my throat after I answer the call. "Don G, how are you?"

"How am I?" He's pissed. I should've called in sooner. "How the fuck do you think I am? You've been gone for three fucking days and I haven't heard a goddamn word. Where's my daughter?"

"She's here. I have her. I mean, I'm with her. We're having dinner right now."

There's a pause. "You're having fucking dinner. I can hear the goddamn ocean in the background. So what? You turn this into a romantic getaway? That's *my fucking daughter* you're with. You touch her, I will cut your balls off. Believe it."

And I guess that answers my question about how Don G feels about me dating his princess.

I'm so fucked.

I resist the urge to clear my throat again. "She doesn't want to come home." It's a lame excuse—I don't know why I even try it.

"I don't give a shit if she wants to come home or not. She's had her fun. Now it's time to get her ass back to Chicago. I'm not having my daughter playing *Girls Gone Wild* down there after the world of trouble she just caused me."

"Of course not. I know. I was just giving her a couple of days to get used to the idea."

"Tell her her mother's going nuts, she's so worried about her. Tell her her grandmother's sick. And you tell her I told Nico Tacone to shut off her spending cash. She has no choice—*she's coming home.*"

"I told her there'd be no retribution when she gets there." I'm not about to bring my girl back if Don G's going to punish her.

"Yeah, right," he grumbles. "No retribution. When did I ever come down on that girl? I never did." He's just complaining now—there's no ire in it. And I believe him.

From what I saw, Jenna was always treated like a mafia princess, except for the marriage contract.

"I'll get her home. By the end of the week—I promise."

"No. Stop fucking around out there. I want her home by tomorrow, end of discussion. *Capiche?*"

My jaw's so tight I think it will break. *"Capisco,"* I mutter.

~

*Jenna*

WHEN ALEX GETS BACK my stomach twists up in a knot. I can tell by the look on his face everything's changed. There's a deadness behind his eyes, resolution in the set of his jaw.

So I was right. Whatever game Alex was playing with me, it's over now. He's doing a job for my father, and it just got called in.

"Let me guess," I say when he sits down, to let him off the hook. "That was my father and he wants me home on the next plane."

Alex purses his lips. "Pretty much, yeah."

"And if I refuse?"

The dead eyes meet mine. A shiver runs down my spine. Who knows the things Alex has done for my father? What crimes or violence he's committed that take the life right out of his soul? He shoves a hand through his dark hair.

"He also forbade me touching you."

I feel like someone slapped me. The contract with Tacone may be off, but my dad still thinks he can control my love life. And of course Alex isn't going to fight him. He can't. In fact, Alex could be in real trouble. That thought pulls me out of my own selfish snit. "Right. Yeah. I won't say anything."

"Jenna, I have to bring you back. It's my j—"

Oh, fuck this. I stand up and toss my napkin on the table. "I know—it's your job. My dad is boss, so whatever he says goes. I guess I thought—" I stop, pressing my lips together to keep them from trembling.

Alex throws American cash on the table and stands up, too. "Thought what, baby?"

I shake my head. "Nope. Not your baby. Never mind. I was wrong." I leave, even though I know without a shadow of a doubt he'll be right behind me.

"Wrong about what, Jenna?" If I didn't know better, I'd swear I hear panic in Alex's voice as he follows me out.

I ignore him, walking swiftly up the beach. This is the last time I'll feel the squish of sand beneath my feet. Tomorrow Alex will drag me back to the Windy City. No more morning walks, no more carefree days.

I don't entertain the idea of running away—not even for a minute. Alex isn't going to let me out of his sight. And even if I did manage to get away, he'd find me. I'm not stupid. I know the only reason my dad didn't send him sooner was because it suited him and business to have me gone for a while.

I shouldn't be pissed at Alex. I knew going into this he was doing a job. I knew he's a player. And yet I still let myself get lulled into imagining we were starting a relationship. We were building something special, something unique.

"Jenna." He grips my elbow and whirls me around.

When I shake his hand off my arm with anger, he releases it so fast you'd think I burned him. He holds his palms out. "Jenna, I'm sorry. Tell me what's going on in your head. You're mad because I didn't listen? Because you have plans and you shared them with me and I'm still bringing you back?"

Okay, no. That's not why I'm mad, but I'm actually kinda softened by the fact that he thinks that's it. It means he *did* listen.

"No." I shake my head. "I'm not mad at you. I just don't want to go."

*"Bullshit."*

Damn. Alex's way of calling bullshit probably scares grown men into peeing themselves. There's so much force and anger behind the word, it's a wonder I don't flinch. Or maybe I do, I'm not sure. I'm trying too hard not to cry.

But there's no way I'm going to confess to him my real woes here. He has an inflated enough ego—he doesn't need to know that I fell head over heels for him and I'm crushed to be reminded that he's here because my father sent him, not for anything more.

"Just leave me alone." I start marching back to the hotel again.

"Jenna, hold up." He arrives by my side, matching my swift pace. "I'm sorry. I'll help you out when we're back in Chicago—set you up with your own place—anything you need. Just because you're going back doesn't mean you have to live at home or give up on your dreams."

I stop, because his gesture is unbelievably sweet, even though it's not the one I wanted. My nose burns, but I manage to hold back my tears. "Thanks, Alex. That's kind of you."

"Yeah?" He ducks his head, trying to peer in my face. It's dark, though, and the moon is just a sliver.

"Yeah, thanks. I'm sorry I got mad. This isn't your fault. It never was."

He slips an arm around my waist, but I dance away again. When we get to my suite and he follows me in, his brows are down, eyes troubled.

Well, too bad. I'm the mystery he's not going to solve tonight.

Or any other night. I had a nice hookup with Alex. He was the perfect guy to lose my virginity with, but if I want to keep my heart from getting crushed any further, I'd better keep my distance.

# CHAPTER 6

 *lex*

I'T's the longest fucking plane trip in the history of the universe. Or maybe just the most miserable. Jenna won't talk. She's not giving me the silent treatment—no, she's quite polite. But there's no friendly chatter. No making conversation.

And she definitely doesn't want to be touched. She skitters away from me every time I lay a hand on her waist or touch her hand.

My stomach churns on the flight home, trying to figure out what I missed. Is Jenna really afraid of her father? I don't think so. But what, then?

We finally land in O'Hare and Don G, himself, picks us up. He acts like he didn't just bust my balls and slaps me on the back, thanking me for bringing his baby home.

I'm relieved to see Jenna's affectionate with him, and he with her, so nothing seems amiss there.

"Well, I'll just get a cab," I tell Don G.

"You sure? I got no problem taking you home."

"Yeah, I'm sure." I cut my glance to Jenna. She's sick of me trailing her by now, and could probably use some space.

Oddly, she doesn't looked relieved.

In fact, she looks like she wants to cry. I touch her elbow. "Hey. Take care of yourself, okay?"

She blinks rapidly on her way in for a hug. "You too." She sounds choked up.

Her dad takes her bag and puts his arm around her shoulders, pulling her against him as they walk away. For some reason, I feel like I'm bleeding out of a giant, gutting wound.

And that's when it hits me like a bullet between the eyes—Jenna's heart was in play.

And I fucking crushed it.

I'm so sick I want to throw up. Somehow my feet still move me to the line of cabs and I make it home, where I throw myself on the bed and stare at the ceiling.

I'm tired and jet-lagged and I can't even trust my own head. All I know is what's in my gut, which feels like a knife twisting and spinning.

Did I read the signs right? Does Jenna care about me? If so, what I did was unconscionable. I took the girl's virginity and walked away, for Christ's sake. What must she think about me?

But what fucking choice did I have? Don Giuseppe

told me to keep my hands off her. If he finds out what I've done, there'll be hell to pay.

Since sleep seems impossible, I get up and stagger to the bathroom to splash water on my face. I can't stand the guy I see looking back at me in the mirror. The guy who hurt Jenna Pachino.

How could I?

And I have no fucking clue how to fix this. Truthfully, she's better off without me. I don't want her to live a life like my mom, always afraid of losing the man she loves. It's not fair to her. She should have her chance to get out of *La Cosa Nostra*.

So just letting the cards lie seems like the best option, if I truly care for her.

Why then, do I still feel like someone's screwing a giant bolt right through the center of me?

*Jenna*

THREE DAYS and I still can't stop moping around the house. I won't even let my mom coax me out for retail therapy. She's in my bedroom for the umpteenth time, trying to get me to talk.

"Baby, please. Tell me what's wrong. Did something happen to you in Spain? Something bad?"

I shake my head. "No, Mom. I just didn't want to come back. I want some time alone."

Downstairs I hear the sound of masculine voices. I

don't even realize my instantaneous reaction of going still, listening for the deep familiar baritone. But it's not him. It's not Alex.

Unfortunately, my interest wasn't missed. My mom gives me a penetrating look. "Something happened with Alex." She says it like a statement, not a question.

My flush gives me away.

She scoots closer to me on the bed. "Did you and he...?"

I swallow and nod.

Her mouth drops open. Then she draws herself up, squares her shoulders. "Well, where is he, then? He hasn't called or stopped by—"

"Dad forbade him to touch me." I don't know why I'm defending him. I had all the same thoughts as my mother. I just can't stand to have anyone think anything bad about —Christ, it's true—the man I love.

My mother's lips press together. "That's ridiculous," she says primly.

"And he's just Dad's puppet, I guess. So that's that."

My mother mutters something in Italian, then stands up and folds her arms across her chest. "No," she says. "Your father doesn't get to decide this for you. Not after he hamstrung you all these years with that farce of a marriage contract. No, he gets absolutely no say in who his daughter dates or doesn't date."

I'm not sure whether to throw up or hug her. "What do you mean, *farce* of a marriage contract?" Because it sure as hell felt real to me.

My mother makes a scoffing sound. "I knew he would

58

never make you go through with it in the end. It was to keep pressure on the Tacones—it wasn't real."

The stone in my stomach grows heavier. "It was real. My whole life you told me I had to marry him. Why would you say that if it wasn't real?"

Suddenly, unexpectedly, my mother bursts into tears.

I stand up, bewildered. She throws her arms around my neck and hugs me tight. "Oh, Jenna. I'm so sorry. It was so wrong, so unfair. I couldn't get your father to end it. He let it go way too far. Until we lost you."

I pat her back, holding back my own tears. Of course my mother suffered as much as I did. She's dedicated her life to me. I'm her only child.

"Jenna!" Alex's voice booms from downstairs. "Jenna?" He repeats my name, but it's closer now, like he's coming up here.

My mom hurriedly pulls away from me and we stare at each other.

"What the fuck is going on?" My dad sounds pissed.

"I need to talk to Jenna." Alex is right outside my door now.

I throw it open. Alex looks terrible—dark circles under his eyes, his hair unkempt, like he's been shoving his fingers through it.

"Anything you need to say to her, you can say to me first." My dad's right behind Alex.

Alex's lips tighten. He stops and pivots to face my father. "Okay." He drags out the second syllable. "Don Giuseppe. I love your daughter—always have. And I think she cares about me, too."

My dad's eyes narrow.

59

I'm frozen, my legs rooted where I stand.

"My daughter's not dating a soldier," my father says flatly.

"I agree," Alex says.

I can't breathe.

"That's why I'm going into investing. See, there's this great fashion styling plan your daughter came up with, and I'd like to fund it."

"Alex," I croak, forcing my body to move forward. I fall into his arms, my cheek pressing up against his hard muscled chest.

"You let them go," my mother demands, poking my father in the chest. "Both of them. Set them free from *La Cosa Nostra*. I don't want my grandchildren living this way."

My father's breathing hard through his nose, so heavy I start to worry he's having a heart attack. I wouldn't be surprised if the cigars and bourbon finally did him in. He lifts a finger and points it at Alex.

Alex doesn't flinch. I'm not surprised, because he is a badass in his own right now, too, but it still takes *palle*.

"You ever hurt her, you cheat on her, I'll cut your motherfucking balls off." My dad sounds so mean, it takes us all a moment to realize he's just conceded.

"Dad," I choke, tears spearing my eyes. I leave Alex's arms to hug him. "I love you," I say to his collar as he squeezes me tight.

"Go on," he grouches, pushing me back in Alex's direction.

"*Lo prometto*," Alex vows, his face as serious as I've ever seen it. He and my father shake hands and my father pulls him in for double cheek kisses.

"Go on," he repeats, slapping Alex's back.

Alex takes my hand. "Come on, baby." He leads down the stairs.

I'm wearing yoga pants and a thin t-shirt, and no makeup. "Where are we going?"

"I don't know. Anywhere you wanna go," he says, leading me out the front door. We get to his car and he pushes me up against the door, slamming his lips down on mine. The kiss has traces of desperation—desire so demanding I'm sure he'll devour me.

When he breaks it off, his eyes are haunted. "Is this what you want? Or did you just get pushed into another future you didn't choose for yourself?"

My lashes moisten. "It's what I want, stupid."

Alex captures the back of my head, his tongue sweeping into my mouth. "Careful, *bambina*," he says when he pulls back. "Or Daddy's going to spank that delicious ass of yours." He claims my mouth again, lips twisting over mine.

"I'm counting on it," I murmur.

# EPILOGUE

*lex*

"ANGEL?" I loosen my tie as I walk in the door of the apartment Jenna and I share.

"In here, Daddy," she calls from the bedroom.

I'm not out of the family business. It's never that easy. Once you're in *La Famiglia*, the only way out is a box. That's what they say, anyway. But Don G and I have an agreement. I got moved to peripheral operations. Nothing too dangerous. Nothing too risky. Following Nico Tacone's example of taking things legal.

In the meantime, I set up an office for Jenna and hired a marketing manager to help her grow her business. She already has three hundred clients from her Facebook ads, and we're working on strategies to get more profit out of the business. Basically, her business model needs to be scaled for mass delivery. She's going to put together set clothing wardrobes for each of the twelve waist placements in three different budgets for each season, and then we'll mass market it that way.

It's a learning and growth process but always fun.

I push open the bedroom door and my breath catches.

Jenna's naked, kneeling in the center of the bed, waiting for me—just like I instructed her.

It's almost too much.

She's so fucking beautiful. So receptive. So obedient.

Which doesn't mean I don't find every excuse in the book to spank her ass cherry red. She loves it as much as I do.

"Good girl," I praise as I walk toward her, pulling the necktie off. "Have you been good all day?"

"Yes, Daddy."

"Well, that deserves a reward." I take her wrists and wind the tie around them, then climb over her, pushing her to her back. I secure the tie to the bedpost.

For a moment I just look at the picture she makes—so beautiful, her chest moving up and down with her rapid breath, her naked body trussed up and ready for me.

I'm definitely going to take care of her. She's my girl. The only person in this world who really knows me. Who I can be myself with. Soon I'm going to ask her to marry me. I already bought the ring. But tonight—tonight is for pleasure.

"Spread your knees, *piccolina*." I tell her, letting every wicked thought I'm having show on my face. "Daddy's going to make you scream."

## The End

THANK you for reading **Mafia Daddy**, a bonus book in the Vegas Underground series.

I am so grateful to you! If you enjoyed this short story, I would so appreciate your review. They make a huge difference for indie authors like me.

Please check out the first three books in the series, **King of Diamonds**, **Jack of Spades**, **Ace of Hearts!** Make sure you're signed up for my newsletter to get word of the release of **Joker's Wild**, Junior and Desiree's story (coming February 2, 2019).

—**SIGN up for my mailing list**: http://owned.gr8.com.

--**Get text alerts of my new releases** by Texting: EZLXP55001 to 474747

--**Join Renee's Romper Room**, my Facebook reader group by emailing me with the email you use for Facebook. It's a secret group (because we discuss kink) so I have to send you an invite to join.

# WANT MORE? JOKER'S WILD - CHAPTER ONE

*Desiree*

My instincts never warned me.

Maybe they would've if I hadn't just worked a twelve hour nursing shift in Trauma. Maybe I wouldn't have just plodded out to my parking garage, brushing off the security guard's offer to walk me to my car.

But I barely notice my surroundings as I walk, keys in hand, to my newly repaired fourteen-year-old Honda Civic. I don't see the shiny black Range Rover parked a few spaces down.

Not until two big guys in trench coats get out of it and come right for me.

*Oh God. This is it. I'm about to be raped and killed.*

I freeze for one second, heart pounding, then dart forward, racing to jump in my car before they can reach me.

"Hold it!" One of them yells and they both lunge, one blocking my driver's side door, the other coming after me.

I open my mouth to scream, but the guy claps a hand over my mouth. "Quiet." His terse command comes out deep and scratchy. He smells of cigar smoke.

Adrenaline pumps through my veins. I know what they say. If someone drags you to a car, you're not going to come back alive, so fight for your life. I elbow my kidnapper, turn my head to bite his hand.

But it's useless. He mutters a curse in some other language and tightens his hold, but otherwise, all my weight thrown around, all my twisting and writhing is nothing to him. He picks me up and carries me forward.

His buddy comes up behind us and presses a gun to my ribs. "Enough with the struggling. Get in the car." They haul me into the back of the Range Rover, sandwiched between the two men and it takes off.

A bag drops over my head and I renew my struggle, but they control me easily, each one taking a wrist and pinning them down by my sides.

"Yeah, we got her," one of them says. At first I think he's talking to the driver, stating the obvious, but then I realize he must be on a phone. "See you there."

"Wh-what's going on?" I warble.

No one answers me.

The phone call gives me pause. They wouldn't call someone to say they had me if their intent was to rape and kill, would they?

*They would if they're devil worshippers who require a virgin sacrifice.*

Not that I'm a virgin. Or that my theory is likely.

68

"I don't know what you want, but, please. Please let me go."

Again, no one bothers answering me.

The Range Rover drives fast--rolling through stops or red lights, making me plow into the men beside me on the turns.

It goes on long enough for me to get good and scared. For my breath to shudder in and out on silent sobs. No tears, though. I must be too afraid to let go.

And then we stop. The asshole on my right drags me out of the car, and I stumble for my footing in the blackness of the sack over my head.

The surroundings are quieter--not a city street any more, but still a sidewalk under my feet.

"What the fuck are you doing?" An angry male voice demands in a low voice, drawing closer with each word. "I told you not to hurt her."

"She's not hurt, just scared." The voice beside me is low, too. We're someplace people would hear us if they raised their voices. A neighborhood?

"Let her go." The bag flies off my head.

I open my mouth to scream, but the sound dies on my lips when I see a face I recognize. I blink up at the pair of sharp, dark eyes above the stubbled masculine line of a powerful jaw belonging to my former employer. Junior Tacone.

Shit. Junior Tacone--acting head of the Tacone crime family.

My galloping heart slows, reverses direction, takes off again.

*"Junior."*

I call him by the name his mother used, forgetting the "Mr. Tacone," forgetting to show respect.

And then, because I had actually been attracted to this man last time I saw him, had thought maybe he had a thing for me, too, and I just had the shit scared out of me, I slap his face, hard.

The men beside me growl and grasp my arms again.

"Let her go." He takes my forearms instead, pulling me into him. Through his long wool coat, the firmness of his large body presses back at me. His dark gaze is command-ing. Intense. "I'll let that stand, this time. Because they scared you."

A shiver runs up my spine. *He'll let that stand.*

Like ordinarily, there would be consequences for slap-ping the mob boss. Of course there would be.

"Now, come inside, I need your help."

I look up the sidewalk at the huge house illuminated by streetlights. It's not his mother's Victorian brick where I worked for three months as a home healthcare nurse after her hip surgery. Must be his?

I try to pull my wrist from his grasp. "No. You can't just, just... *kidnap* me and tell me to come inside because you need my help."

He shifts his grasp to hold my wrist and tips his head toward the house. "Let's go." He doesn't even bother answering my argument. And I suppose that's because I'm dead wrong. He *can* just kidnap me and demand my help. He's Junior Tacone, of the Chicago underground. He and his men have guns. They can make me do whatever they damn well please.

The relief that trickled in when I saw his handsome

face ebbs back out. I may still never walk out of here. Because whatever awaits me in that house isn't going to be pretty. Or legal.

Someone's hurt and they need a nurse. That's my best guess.

And now I'll be a witness to whatever they're trying to hide.

Are they torturing someone? Need me to keep him alive so they can get something out of him? Or is one of their members hurt?

I have no choice but to go in. I may be considered spunky, but I'm not willing to find out what happens if you defy the kingpin of Chicago.

So I fall into step beside him, hurrying to match his long strides. He slides his grip from my wrist to my hand. His large hand warms my icy one and has a protective quality, like we're on a date.

Like I'm not his prisoner.

# READ ALL THE VEGAS UNDERGROUND BOOKS

***King of Diamonds (Book 1)***

"Dark, dirty, and perfect--Renee Rose has mastered this genre." ~USA Today Bestselling Author Alta Hensley

**I WARNED YOU.**

I told you not to set foot in my casino again. I told you
to stay away. Because if I see those hips swinging around
my suite, I'll pin you against the wall and take you hard.
And once I make you mine, I'm not gonna set you free.
I'm king of the Vegas underground and I take
what I want.

So run. Stay the hell away from my casino.
Or I'll tie you to my bed. Put you on your knees.
Break you.

Or else come to me, beautiful, if you dare...

*Mafia Daddy (in Daddy's Demands) (book 1.5)*

Don G gave me orders--find his daughter, straighten her out, and bring her home. But she's staying with me. Because despite the marriage contract to another family, Jenna Pachino has always been mine.

### Jack of Spades (Book 2)

"Raw, addictive, and absolutely luscious. Renee Rose never fails to deliver!" ~USA Today Bestselling author Jane Henry

### "YOU'RE AT MY MERCY NOW, *AMORE.*"

Sorry, *bella.* You got dealt the losing hand.
Witness to a crime, you're my prisoner now.
I didn't mean for things to happen this way,
But tying you to my bed and making you scream
is an unexpected pleasure. A privilege, really.
And even if I did trust you, now that I've had a taste,
I'm not sure I'd let you go...

### Ace of Hearts (Book 3)

**THE SWEET LITTLE SONGBIRD'S IN MY CAGE NOW.**

She owes the Family money. Big money. And I'm the guy
they sent to put the squeeze on her. So now she's playing at my casino.

Strutting around on my stage in her tight little shorts. Killing me softly.

I promised she'll be treated with respect, so long as she does as she's told.

But I didn't count on her barging in my office and tempting me,

begging for a taste of my authority.

I didn't count on her getting under my skin.

And the last thing I want is to see her debt paid.

Because then I'd have to set her free…

*Joker's Wild (book 5) Coming February 2, 2019*

# ABOUT RENEE ROSE

**USA TODAY BESTSELLING AUTHOR RENEE ROSE** loves a dominant, dirty-talking alpha hero! She's sold over a half million copies of steamy romance with varying levels of kink. Her books have been featured in USA Today's Happily Ever After and Popsugar.

Named Eroticon USA's Next Top Erotic Author in 2013, she has also won *Spunky and Sassy's* Favorite Sci-Fi and Anthology Author, *The Romance Reviews* Best Historical Romance, and *Spanking Romance Reviews'* Best Historical, Best Erotic, Best Ageplay and favorite author. She's hit #1 on Amazon in the Erotic Paranormal, Western and Sci-fi categories.

**Please follow her on:**
  **Bookbub | Goodreads | Instagram**

*Renee loves to connect with readers!*
www.reneeroseromance.com
reneeroseauthor@gmail.com

**Vegas Underground Mafia Romance**

*King of Diamonds (book 1)*

*Jack of Spades (book 2)*

*Ace of Hearts (book 3)*

*Mafia Daddy (book 4)*

*Joker's Wild (book 5) Coming soon*

**More Mafia Romance**

*The Russian*

*The Don's Daughter*

*Mob Mistress*

*The Bossman*

**Contemporary**

*Blaze: A Firefighter Daddy Romance*

*Black Light: Roulette Redux*

*Her Royal Master*

*The Russian*

*Black Light: Valentine Roulette*

*Theirs to Protect*

*Scoring with Santa*

*Owned by the Marine*

*Theirs to Punish*

*Punishing Portia*

*The Professor's Girl*

*Safe in his Arms*

*Saved*

*The Elusive "O"*


**Paranormal**

**Bad Boy Alphas Series**

*Alpha's Secret (coming Jan. 26)*

*Alpha's Bane*

*Alpha's Mission*

*Alpha's War*

*Alpha's Desire*

*Alpha's Obsession*

*Alpha's Challenge*

*Alpha's Prize*

*Alpha's Danger*

*Alpha's Temptation*

*Love in the Elevator (Bonus story to Alpha's Temptation)*


***Alpha Doms Series***

*The Alpha's Hunger*

*The Alpha's Promise*

*The Alpha's Punishment*


**Other Paranormals**

*His Captive Mortal*

*Deathless Love*

*Deathless Discipline*

*The Winter Storm: An Ever After Chronicle*

## Sci-Fi

## Zandian Masters Series

*His Human Slave*

*His Human Prisoner*

*Training His Human*

*His Human Rebel*

*His Human Vessel*

*His Mate and Master*

*Zandian Pet*

Their Zandian Mate

*His Human Possession*

## Zandian Brides (Reverse Harem)

*Night of the Zandians*

*Bought by the Zandians*

*Mastered by the Zandians*

*Zandian Lights*

*The Hand of Vengeance*

*Her Alien Masters*

## Regency

*The Darlington Incident*

*Humbled*

*The Reddington Scandal*

*The Westerfield Affair*

*Pleasing the Colonel*

## Western

*His Little Lapis*

*The Devil of Whiskey Row*

*The Outlaw's Bride*

## Medieval

*Mercenary*

*Medieval Discipline*

*Lords and Ladies*

*The Knight's Prisoner*

*Betrothed*

*Held for Ransom*

*The Knight's Seduction*

*The Conquered Brides (5 book box set)*

## Renaissance

*Renaissance Discipline*

## Ageplay

*Stepbrother's Rules*

*Her Hollywood Daddy*

*His Little Lapis*

*Black Light: Valentine's Roulette (Broken)*


**BDSM under the name Darling Adams**

**Medical Play**

*Yes, Doctor*

**Master/Slave**

*Punishing Portia*

Made in the USA
Middletown, DE
06 June 2023

32144500R00054